ANIMAL VS. ANIMAL

WHO'S THE BRIGHTEST?

BY EMILIE DUFRESNE

Please visit our website, www.garethstevens.com. For a free color catalog of all our high-quality books, call toll free 1-800-542-2595 or fax 1-877-542-2596.

Cataloging-in-Publication Data

Title: Who's the brightest? / Emilie Dufresne.
Description: New York : Gareth Stevens Publishing, 2022. | Series: Animal vs. animal | Includes glossary and index.
Identifiers: ISBN 9781534537385 (pbk.) | ISBN 9781534537408 (library bound) | ISBN 9781534537392 (6 pack) | ISBN 9781534537415 (ebook)
Subjects: LCSH: Animal intelligence--Juvenile literature. | Cognition in animals--Juvenile literature. | Animal behavior--Juvenile literature.
Classification: LCC QL785.D843 2022 | DDC 591.5'13--dc23

Published in 2022 by
Gareth Stevens Publishing
29 East 21st Street
New York, NY 10010

© 2022 Booklife Publishing
This edition is published by arrangement with Booklife Publishing

Edited by: John Wood
Designed by: Danielle Rippengill

All rights reserved. No part of this book may be reproduced in any form without permission in writing from the publisher, except by a reviewer.

Printed in the United States of America

Some of the images in this book illustrate individuals who are models. The depictions do not imply actual situations or events.

CPSIA compliance information: Batch #CSGS22: For further information contact Gareth Stevens, New York, New York at 1-800-542-2595.

Find us on

IMAGE CREDITS

All images are courtesy of Shutterstock.com, unless otherwise specified. With thanks to Getty Images, Thinkstock Photo, and iStockphoto. Cover – Ovocheva, Stepova Oksana, Abscent, StockSmartStart, Nutkins J, Nadzin, StudioLondon. Images used on every page – Ovocheva, Stepova Oksana. 5 – ONYXprj, Abscent. 6 – Alyona28, Nutkins J. 7 – Nadzin, StudioLondon. 6&7 – StockSmartStart, Guingm. 8 – Jan Bures, Alyona28. 9 – reptiles4all. 8&9 – Guingm. 10 – Alyona28. 10&11 – Abscent. 12 – Nutkins J, Anton Dzyna, Jurgen Otto [CC BY-SA 2.0 (https://creativecommons.org/licenses/by-sa/2.0)], via Wikimedia Commons. 13 – Nadzin, StudioLondon, Drop of Light. 12&13 – Guingm. 14 – Nutkins J. 15 – Nadzin, StudioLondon. 14&15 – Abscent. 16 – MOreJOy. 17 – Giedriius. 16&17 – Guingm, StockSmartStart. 18&19 – Abscent, StockSmartStart. 20&21 – amiloslava. 22 – Guingm. 23 – Abscent.

CONTENTS

PAGE 4   The Great and Small Games

PAGE 6   The Contenders

PAGE 8   Chameleon vs. Garter Snake

PAGE 10   The Color Count

PAGE 12   Peacock Spider vs. Peacock

PAGE 14   Dance-Off

PAGE 16   Macaw vs. Peacock Butterfly

PAGE 18   Best Photograph

PAGE 20   Hall of Fame

PAGE 22   Quiz and Activity

PAGE 24   Glossary and Index

Words that look like this can be found in the glossary on page 24.

THE GREAT AND SMALL GAMES

Step right up!
It's the Great and Small Games!
See nature's brightest and most beautiful creatures!

Today's events:
The Color Count!
Dance-Off!
Best Photograph!

These events will surely decide once and for all:
Who's the Brightest?

THE CONTENDERS

Let's find out some facts and figures about today's contenders!

Panther Chameleon
The Ravishing Rainbow

Size: Up to 20 inches (50.8 cm)

Lives: Madagascar, Réunion Island, and Mauritius

Beauty Trick: Color-changing skin

Peacock Butterfly
The Fancy Flutterer

Size: Up to 3 inches (7.6 cm)

Lives: Europe and Asia

Beauty Trick: Patterned wings

Peacock Spider
The Tiny Dancer

Size: Around 0.16 inch (4 mm)

Lives: Australia

Beauty Trick: Colorful dance moves

Macaw
Feathered and Fabulous

Size: Around 3 feet (1 m) including tail

Lives: South and Central America

Beauty Trick: Brightly-colored feathers

Red-Sided Garter Snake
Stripes (Are Always in Style)

Size: Around 3.3 feet (1 m)

Lives: North America and Canada, near woodlands and water

Beauty Trick: Long, colored stripes

Peacock
Loud and Proud

Size: Up to 3.8 feet (1.2 m) from beak to tail...and up to 7.4 feet (2.3 m) with **train**!

Lives: Southeast Asia, India, and the Congo basin

Beauty Trick: Displays of its beautiful train

7

CHAMELEON VS.

Rrrrrround Onnnne!

I'M CHANGING COLOR!

This **flamboyant** reptile looks like a colorful rainbow and knows it! With the ability to change colors right in front of your eyes, this lizard is not afraid to stand out in a crowd.

Nickname:
The Ravishing Rainbow

Top Tip:
Always **accessorize**. Chameleons never leave home without their very long tongues and amazing eyesight.

GARTER SNAKE

This stripy snake has style, sass, and swagger! With a mixture of spots and stripes, this Californian creature is the most fashion-forward reptile out there!

Nickname:
Stripes (Are Always in Style)

Top Tip:
Color where you can. Even a garter snake's tongue is red with a black part at the end.

Garter snakes are silent and can't even hiss! They let their look speak for itself.

TRUSST IN MY SSTYLE!

THE COLOR COUNT

It's a counting contest to decide who's the brightest out of these multicolored masterpieces. Let's get counting and see what they've got!

First up: the chameleon...

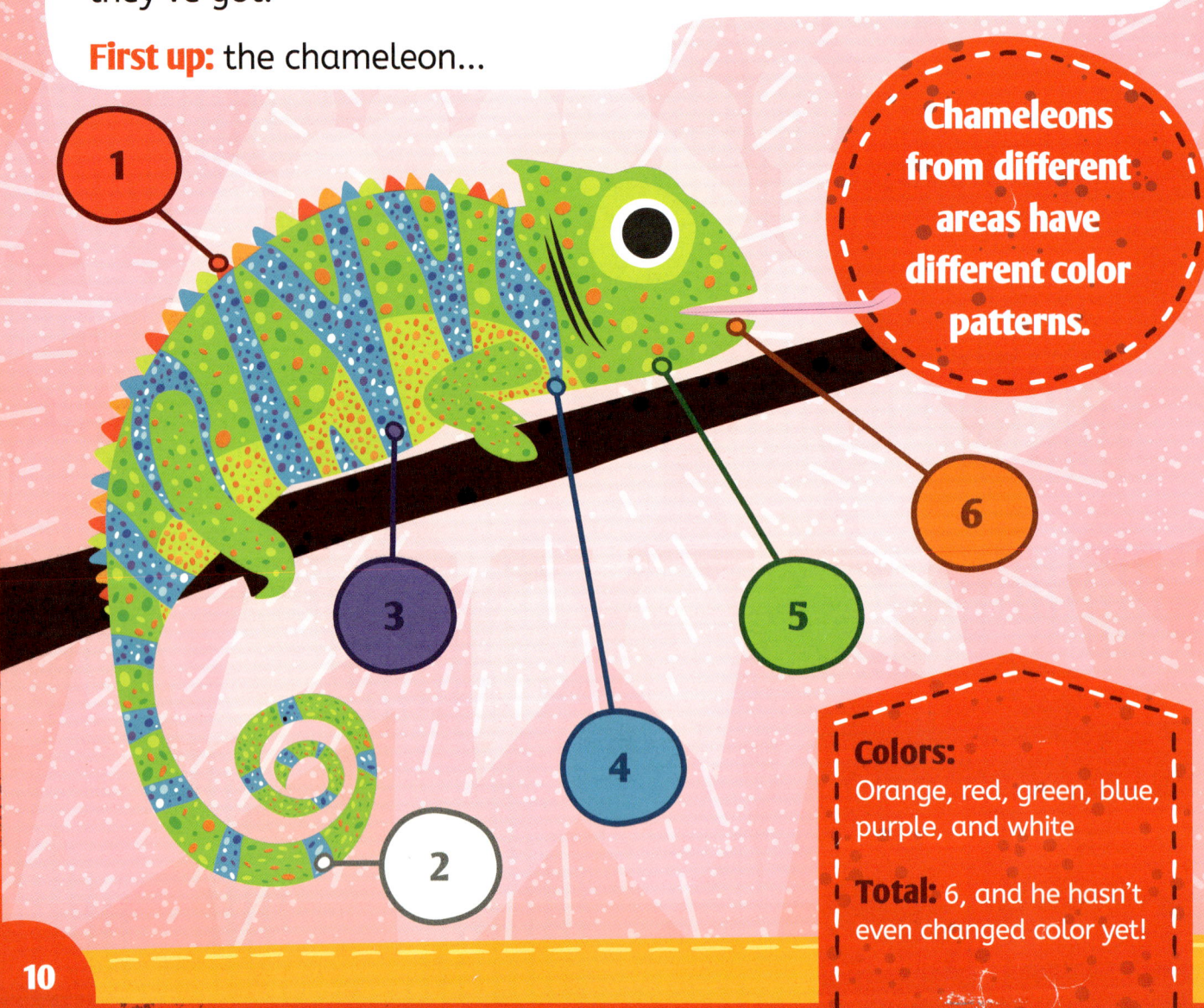

Chameleons from different areas have different color patterns.

Colors:
Orange, red, green, blue, purple, and white

Total: 6, and he hasn't even changed color yet!

Now for our **second contender:** the garter snake.

Colors:
Blue, red, and black

Total: 3

The garter snake may be bold and brilliantly patterned, but it's not enough to win this round!

Round one goes to the **panther chameleon!**

11

PEACOCK SPIDER

Rrrrrrround Twoooo!

SHAKE IT!

This spider may be a tiny dancer, but he has some big moves! With his multicolored **abdomen** and awesome arm movements, this little guy will get everyone up and dancing.

Nickname:
The Tiny Dancer

Top Tip:
Always exit with drama and style. Why walk when you can **sashay**?

VS. PEACOCK

This peacock has got some serious **plumage** and he's ready to use it. His fantastic fan of feathers will be sure to put you in a dance trance.

Nickname:
Loud and Proud

Top Tip:
Be "prop-pared." Always have a fan at hand to give your dance that dramatic flair.

Peacocks have a pattern on their feathers that looks like many eyes staring back at you.

WOW AH AH!

DANCE-OFF

It's time to see how these two get down and show off their colors in the talent contest. Let's put the music on and see who can shake a tail feather (or abdomen) the best...

A peacock spider's dance can last for up to 50 minutes. They must have great stamina!

Does anyone else feel dizzy? All the colors, they are just so pretty and dazzling. Who was the first contestant again... Round two goes to the **peacock!**

A peacock's tail is around 5 feet (1.5 m) long!

MACAW VS.

Rrrrrrround Threee!

BWARK!

It's not only this big bird's mouth that is loud – its feathers are too! This magnificent macaw is ready to show off its vivid colors and tail and strut its stuff.

Nickname:
Feathered and Fabulous

Top Tip:
Never be afraid to put lots of different bright colors together.

PEACOCK BUTTERFLY

This gentle gem will blow you away with just one flap of its wings. Just like a peacock, its eye-shaped patterns will dazzle you. What an incredible insect!

Nickname:
The Fancy Flutterer

Top Tip:
Practice useful fashion. This butterfly's pattern protects him from **predators** as well as looking great!

When looked at upside down, a peacock butterfly's wings look like the face of an owl.

FLAP!

BEST PHOTOGRAPH

Okay, contestants, it's time to see who can take the best photograph. Strike a pose and show off your colors to get the best picture.

Every macaw has a different feather pattern on its face.

HALL OF FAME

Keel-Billed Toucan
Known for their big, bright beaks.

Lives: Central America

Eats: Fruit, insects, and eggs

Color: Multicolored

Agama Lizard
Also known as the Spider-Man lizard, they can make themselves red and blue.

Lives: Africa

Eats: Insects, grass, and berries

Color: Bright red and blue

Flamingo
Looking pretty in pink, these birds are colored by what they eat.

Lives: Worldwide

Eats: **Algae**, crustaceans, and fish

Color: Pink

Peacock Mantis Shrimp
These brightly colored **crustaceans** (say: crus-TAY-shuns) are covered in a lovely leopard-spot pattern.

Lives: Tropical waters in the Indian and Pacific Oceans

Eats: Crabs, shrimps, and snails

Color: Multicolored

QUIZ AND...

Now you know about the animals and how bright they can be! Can you get all these questions right? Let's have a look and see!

Questions

1. What size is the peacock spider?

2. How many colors does the red-sided garter snake have?

3. What pattern do the peacock's feathers have on them?

4. What does the peacock mantis shrimp eat?

5. What animal does a peacock butterfly's wings look like upside down?

6. How long can a peacock spider's dance last?

ACTIVITY

Just like the peacock and the spider, learning a dance routine can give you a great way to show off your clothes. Let's try to learn one.

1. Right Arm Up
2. Both Arms Up
3. Jump to the Left
4. Right Arm Down

Don't forget to shake it!

Answers from page 22: 1. 0.16 inch 2. 3 colors 3. Lots of eyes 4. Crabs, shrimps, and snails 5. An owl's 6. 50 minutes

GLOSSARY

abdomen — the part of a body that contains reproductive and digestive organs
accessorize — to add extra things to an outfit, such as jewelry, a bag, or a hat
algae — a plant or plantlike living thing that has no roots, stems, leaves, or flowers
crustacean — a type of animal that lives in water and has a hard outer shell
flamboyant — bold and colorful
plumage — the pattern, color, and layout of a bird's feathers
predator — an animal that hunts other animals for food
sashay — to walk with swinging hip movements in order to look fabulous
stamina — the ability to be able to do something for a long time
train — something long and flowing at the back of something, such as an animal or a piece of clothing

INDEX

bright 4–5, 7, 10, 16, 20–22
butterfly 6, 17, 19
chameleon 6, 8, 10–11
color 4–12, 14–16, 18–22
crustaceans 21
dance 4, 6, 12–14, 22–23
fashion 9, 17
lizards 20
multicolored 10, 12, 20–21
patterns 6, 10–11, 13, 17–18, 21–22
peacock 7, 13, 15, 23